The
Jelly
Bean
Tree

for
Liz Szabla

A FEIWEL AND FRIENDS BOOK
An imprint of Macmillan Publishing Group, LLC

THE JELLY BEAN TREE. Copyright © 2017 by Toni Yuly.
All rights reserved.
Printed in China by RR Donnelley Asia Printing Solutions Ltd.,
Dongguan City, Guangdong Province. For information,
address Feiwel and Friends, 175 Fifth Avenue, New York, N.Y. 10010.

Our books may be purchased in bulk for promotional, educational,
or business use. Please contact your local bookseller or the Macmillan Corporate
and Premium Sales Department at (800) 221-7945 ext. 5442 or by e-mail at
MacmillanSpecialMarkets@macmillan.com.

Library of Congress Cataloging-in-Publication Data is available.
ISBN 978-1-250-09406-3

Book design by Anna Booth
Feiwel and Friends logo designed by Filomena Tuosto

First Edition—2017

The artwork was created using torn tissue paper, twine, cut and torn
construction paper, pen and ink, and digital collage.

10 9 8 7 6 5 4 3 2 1

mackids.com

The Jelly Bean Tree

Toni
Yuly

FEIWEL AND FRIENDS   NEW YORK

Jelly Bean has

long
legs,

a

long

tail . . .

. . . and a
very
long
neck.

Jelly Bean's favorite place

is with the trees.

She especially loves
to nap with them.

One day, Jelly Bean took a

long,

long . . . .

looong

long

nap.

When she woke up,
she heard something.

"I hope my nest
won't fall!" chirped
Mama Bird.

Jelly Bean
stood
very
still
for the
rest of the
day . . .

and
night.

The next morning,
Jelly Bean's friends
came by.

"What are
you doing?"
asked Dog.

"I am a tree,"
said Jelly Bean. "See my nest?"

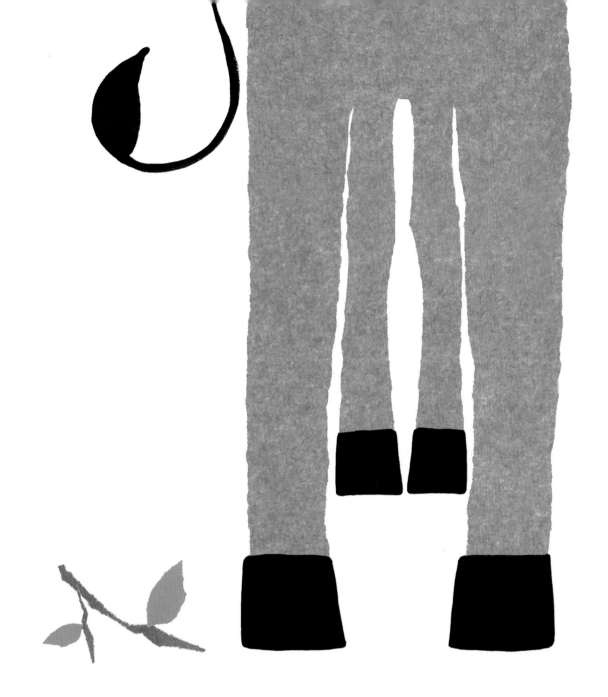

"Oh," said Dog. "That's nice.
How long will you be a tree?"

"I don't know," said Jelly Bean.
"I have never been a tree before."

As the days passed . . .

Jelly Bean's friends
brought her snacks . . .

. . . and picked
her some flowers.

They played . . .

but not too hard.

"How much longer
will you be a tree?"
asked Turtle.

Jelly Bean
wasn't sure.

And then . . .

peep
peep
peep

Soon the chicks
were hungry.

And Mama flew off to find food.

"The birds need a different tree now," thought Jelly Bean.

But everyone knew,
there was no tree
better than . . .

the
Jelly Bean
tree.